THE
PLAYGROUND
MEANIES

All about **BEING KIND** with *Pickle & Bree*

By Alison Reynolds

Illustrated by Mikki Butterley

The Five Mile Press

It was a sunny day in the park.
Bree wobbled on her tippy toes.
She stretched and stretched, but she
was still too short for the flying fox.

"Can we have a go?" asked two little bears.
"We're Howard and Gracie."
Bree stepped back. "Sure – if you can reach."
Howard and Gracie grinned.
"Watch this!"

They clambered on and
ZOOMED away.

"Sorry we're late, Bree,' Pickle said breathlessly. "We had a spelling test."
"I took ages," said Jason in his soft bear voice. "Pickle had to wait for me."
Pickle patted Jason's back.
"It's okay. Everybody knows bears aren't good at spelling."

Howard jumped off the flying fox. "Says who? *We* can spell just fine."
Jason hung his head and stared at his feet.

"Whoa!" said Howard.
"Look at your big feet!"

Gracie giggled.
"Pickle and Jason have
big floppy clown feet,"
she sang.

Pickle was confused. "I'm a big bear. I need big feet."
"Jason's feet are even bigger," said Howard with a laugh.

Pickle frowned. He didn't like the sound of Howard's laugh.
"My feet are big enough to kick rude little bear bottoms–"
Bree grabbed Pickle's paw. "Ignore them, Pickle," she whispered.
"You don't want to be mean, too."

Bree pulled Pickle and Jason to the other side of the playground.
"Let's try out the slide," she said.

Pickle clambered up the ladder. "Come on, Jason."
But Jason stood at the bottom, watching Howard and Gracie. They were still
laughing and pointing.
"Cover your ears so you can't hear," said Bree.

"Jason can't climb," shouted Gracie. "His feet are too big for the ladder!"
Howard and Gracie giggled and giggled.

Jason uncovered his ears. "What did they say?"

"Nothing," said Pickle. He glanced helplessly at Bree.

"Come on board the slide, Jason," Bree said quickly.

Jason grunted and squeezed behind Pickle.

Just as he was getting ready to whoosh down the slide, Jason caught a glimpse of something in the sand pit.

Pickle's tummy flipped flopped – but he felt even worse
when he heard Jason's sad sniff.

"Oh, Jason," said Bree. "Do you want us to play Bear Bump to cheer you up?"

Jason's shoulders shook. "I don't think it will help, Bree. It isn't nice to feel like there's something wrong with you."

Pickle was an easy-going bear. But he didn't like it one little bit when his friends were unhappy.

"Nobody's allowed to make Jason sad." Pickle scrunched his face, trying to look fierce and mean. "I'm going to scare them with my biggest bear roar."

Bree shook her head. "But Pickle, if you do that you'll be just as bad as them."

Pickle looked at Jason, who still had big tears plopping down his furry nose.

"Sorry, Bree,' Pickle said firmly. "Cover your ears."

Birds flew out of the trees.
Bunnies dived for their burrows.
And everybody else fled the park.

Bree shivered. "That was the most ferocious roar I've ever heard!"

Pickle glanced at his best friend. Bree looked a little scared.
And Jason didn't look any happier. Suddenly, Pickle felt awful,
even worse than tummy flip-flops.

"I'm sorry," he said.
"I just wanted to help. I thought it
would make me feel better, but now I just feel sadder."

"Hey," shouted Gracie. "Where is everybody?"

Pickle wrinkled his forehead. "Where did you go?"

Howard nodded at his scooter basket. "We went home to get supplies. Honey buns and fresh honey cakes."

Pickle's mouth watered.

"Look Howard – the buns are nearly as big as Jason's feet!"
Gracie snorted with laughter.

Pickle growled. Jason sighed.

Bree's tummy rumbled.
"I wish we had honey buns," she said.

Jason spoke softly in Pickle's ear.

Pickle brightened. "Good idea, Jason!
Maybe we should stand on their
honey buns with our big bear feet."

Bree scowled. "Definitely, not! Trust me, Pickle, that won't make anyone feel better."
She pressed her fingers to her head. "Instead, we should..."

Pickle and Jason waited. Bree was usually full of excellent ideas.

But for once, Bree couldn't think of a single solution.

Jason rubbed his eyes.
"Then they'll tease me and my big feet forever."

Suddenly there was a strange sound, a clunk followed by a hiss.
Pickle and Bree looked around in alarm as a big jet of water shot up from
the park sprinklers.

"Help!" yelled Howard.

"Oh no!" shouted Gracie.

"OUR HONEY CAKES!"
they bellowed together.

Pickle wanted to laugh.

But then he thought about how sad
Jason was just a moment ago.

And then he looked at how
sad Howard and Gracie
were now.

Somehow, he didn't feel
like laughing anymore.

"What should we do, Bree?"
Pickle whispered.

"Jason – use your foot,"
Bree whispered back.

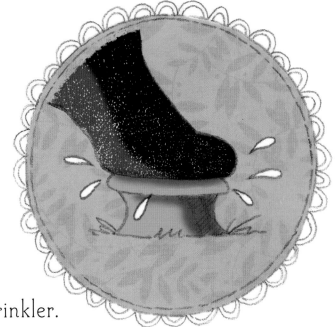

Jason lifted up one big foot
        and pressed down hard on the sprinkler.

The water stopped. Pickle and Bree rescued a few dry honey buns and handed them to Howard and Gracie.

"Thanks," muttered Gracie.

Pickle put a hand behind his ear. "Pardon me?"

Howard took a deep breath. "Thank you, Jason," he said loudly.

Gracie held out a big honey bun.

Jason grinned and whispered in Pickle's ear.

"He said any time," said Pickle loudly.

The sun was setting as Bree
licked the last splodge
of honey from her fingers.

"Yum," she said.
"Just in time for one last slide."

"Hey, Jason?" said Howard shyly.
"Your feet are a little bit like surfboards!"

Jason grinned. "Jump on board."

"See, Pickle?" said Bree. "Wasn't this better than us being mean too?"

Pickle nodded. "You were right, Bree."

Bree cupped her hand behind her ear. "What? I didn't hear that."

Pickle just laughed.

Pickle & Bree's
Guide to Good Deeds

Pickle and Bree always try to be kind –
but sometimes, people are not kind in return.
Pickle and Bree have to work hard to remember
that being mean is never the answer.
Here are Pickle and Bree's tips on being kind:

1. Sometimes, a person might not realise that they are making
    you sad. Try to tell them how you feel. But if they don't
    want to listen, then walk away and find someone who will
    treat you with respect.

2. Some people, for whatever reason, just don't want to be nice.
    It is okay to walk away when someone is mean to you.

3. Tell an adult if someone is being unkind. They can often
    help, but if they can't, keep telling other adults until you
    find somebody who will help you.

4. Sometimes, a bully's only goal is to see that they
    have made you sad. It's not always easy to ignore
    them, but if they don't think they are succeeding,
    they may give up.

5. Remember, it is not your fault if someone
    is unkind to you. Nobody has the right
    to make you feel bad about yourself.
    You are okay just the way you are!